CELEBI

Based on "The

ADAPTED BY

SCHOLASTIC INC.

New York   Toronto   London   Auckland   Sydney
Mexico City   New Delhi   Hong Kong   Buenos Aires

ISBN-13: 978-0-545-00560-9
ISBN-10: 0-545-00560-4

Published by Scholastic Inc.
SCHOLASTIC and associated logos are trademarks and/or registered trademarks of Scholastic Inc.

12 11 10 9 8 7 6 5 4   8 9 10 11 12/0

Designed by Cheung Tai
Printed in the U.S.A.

First printing, June 2007

Celebi . . . Lost!

Deep in the forest of the Battle Frontier, a fire raged.

Angry flames leaped into the sky, consuming every tree and bush in its path.

The fire grew hotter and hotter. For the Pokémon of the forest, there was no escape. They gathered together, trapped between walls of flame. Small Oddish trembled next to a bunch of pink Exeggcute. Crawling Caterpie and majestic Stantler huddled together. Even Flying-types like Butterfree, Beedrill, and Spearow were trapped. They couldn't fly through the thick smoke.

The flames grew closer. It looked like all hope was lost.

Then a small green Pokémon flew toward the flames. Celebi's round head was pale green and shaped like a plant bulb. Small transparent wings flapped on its green back. It scanned the flames with two big blue eyes, and its entire body began to glow with green light.

The huddled Pokémon spotted Celebi in the sky. They watched, suddenly filled with hope.

Celebi fearlessly flew right into the flames. But the Pokémon was not harmed. The flames immediately transformed into green, thorny vines. Celebi's glow spread throughout the forest, until every flame was transformed.

The thick vines would have choked the forest. But seconds after they formed, they dissolved into droplets of light. These droplets rose up into the air, and then vanished.

Celebi flew to the forest floor, exhausted. It looked around at the burned and blackened trees. The forest needed healing. But Celebi needed to gather energy first.

Suddenly, one of the burned trees cracked in half. It toppled over onto Celebi!

The Pokémon did not have much time to act. As the crushing weight of the tree came down, Celebi used its special ability. It transported itself to another point in time.

The Forest Pokémon watched in amazement as Celebi vanished. The Pokémon had saved them.

What would happen to their guardian now?

Some time in the future — or was it the past? — Celebi slowly opened its eyes. It was badly hurt. With its last bit of energy, Celebi created more thick vines. The vines grew around Celebi, protecting it.

Then the little Pokémon fainted.

A Strange Detour

Ash Ketchum and his friends were walking down a tree-lined trail through the Battle Frontier. Ash was heading toward the Battle Pike. He was hoping to earn another Frontier Symbol by battling his Pokémon.

Ash's friend Max checked the PokéNav as they walked. Max was the youngest of the group. He wasn't old enough to become a Pokémon Trainer yet. But he was a great navigator. He always knew how to get the friends to their next destination.

"Looks like we'll save time taking the Cycling Road," Max remarked.

Brock, the oldest of the friends, nodded. "The Cycling Road has a bicycle rental as well."

Max's sister, May, liked the idea, too. "Awesome!" she cheered, her blue eyes sparkling. "There's nothing like bicycling on a nice day, you know?"

Ash liked the idea for another reason. "Then I'll get my next Frontier Symbol in no time."

"*Pika!*" agreed Pikachu, Ash's little yellow Pokémon. Pikachu traveled on Ash's shoulder, as usual.

Soon the large gates of the Cycling Road came into view. The man-made road behind it was smooth and paved.

Pikachu pointed at the gate. "*Pika! Pika!*"

Ash squinted. Someone was standing in front of the gate. He couldn't quite see who it was.

But Brock knew right away. He ran toward her.

"Officer Jenny is here!" he cried. He got that dreamy look in his eyes whenever he saw a pretty young woman. Luckily for Brock, almost every town had an identical-looking Officer Jenny.

Max noticed something else. "Something's wrong," he said. He pointed to the barricades in front of the gates.

"The road's closed!" Ash cried.

Officer Jenny smiled at them. "I'm sorry, but there was so much rain last night that we had an awful mudslide," she said. There seemed to be something a little different about her. Her face was stiff, and she spoke in a flat voice.

"There *is* a detour, if you're in a hurry," she continued. She pointed to a dirt trail at the side of the gates. "It's a little bit off the beaten path, but it does lead to Fuschia City."

Ash frowned. "Aw, man. I really wanted to bike."

But the friends had no choice. They had to move on. The dirt trail was rocky and bumpy.

May was suspicious of their new path. Officer

Jenny seemed a little strange. Something else bothered her, too.

"I don't remember last night's storm being that bad, do you?" she asked.

"There's no way it was bad enough to start a mudslide, that's for sure," Max said.

Then Pikachu sat up on Ash's shoulder. Its yellow ears twitched.

"*Pika! Pika!*" it cried urgently.

Pikachu jumped off Ash's shoulder. It ran off the detour onto another path.

"Pikachu!" Ash cried. He ran off after his Pokémon. Brock, May, and Max followed.

"Pikachu, wait!" Ash yelled.

"Where are you going?" Max called out after him.

Suddenly, a young woman jumped in front of them. She held out her arms, blocking their way.

"Hold it!" she yelled.

A Plusle jumped off her shoulder and stood in front of her. Electricity crackled from the red marks on its cheeks.

"Turn back!" the woman cried. "No one's allowed past this point!"

The Pokémon Ranger

"It's a Pokémon Ranger!" Max cried. He could tell from the woman's uniform. She wore gray shorts, tall boots, and a short-sleeved white and red jacket with a gold collar. Her light blue hair was in a ponytail on top of her head.

"You're kidding," Ash and May said together. Pokémon Rangers weren't a common sight. May had never even seen one in person before.

"Please return to the detour road," the Ranger said sternly.

"But my Pikachu just ran off in there!" Ash pleaded.

The Ranger's eyes widened in surprise. "Wait

just a minute," she said. She took a small radio off her belt and spoke into it.

"It's Solana," she said. "We've got a Pikachu over the line. I've also got its Trainer and its Trainer's accomplices attempting pursuit."

Ash was impressed. It all sounded so official.

Finally, Solana nodded. "Understood."

She switched off the radio and looked up at Ash and his friends. "So, what are your names?" she asked.

"I'm Ash from Pallet Town," Ash said.

"My name is May!" May said, smiling.

"And I'm Max," said Max.

Brock ran up to Solana, grasping her hands in his. "And my name is Brock!" he gushed. "I know this place is off-limits, but please don't let your love be as well!"

Max grabbed Brock by the ear and dragged him away from her. "Out of bounds!" he scolded. "Pikachu's not the only one who's over the line."

May and Ash laughed, and Solana smiled.

"Anyway, it's a pleasure to meet you," Solana said. "I'm Solana, and this is Plusle."

Plusle had climbed back onto Solana's shoulder.

"*Plusle! Plusle!*" The little Electric-type Pokémon waved hello.

"The Ranger Union said you could move on," Solana reported. "Follow me!"

She turned and walked down the path that led into the woods. Ash and the others followed.

"Okay, guys, I know this!" Max shouted. Behind his glasses, his dark eyes shone with excitement. "A Pokémon Ranger deals with problems like accidents and natural disasters. Is that right?"

"That's right, Max," Solana said, looking over her shoulder. "With help from wild Pokémon."

"How do the Pokémon Rangers manage that?" Ash wondered.

"That's what I'd like to know," May added.

Suddenly, the path came to an end. Thick, green vines blocked the way, snaking throughout the forest.

"Look at the size of those vines!" Brock exclaimed.

"Pikachu's gotta be in there," Ash said and disappeared into the tangle of vines.

"Ash, wait!" May yelled as she chased after him.

But Ash couldn't get far. The vines got thicker and more twisted the deeper he went. A tiny Pikachu could get through — but not a human. He stopped, and the others caught up to him.

May frowned. "It's too thick."

"There's no way you can get through that," Max remarked.

Solana looked just as determined as Ash. "We have to," she said. "Celebi is in there."

Everyone gasped. Celebi was a Legendary

Pokémon! It wasn't every day you saw one of those.

"The Pokémon they call Guardian of the Forest?" Max couldn't believe it.

Solana took a small device off her belt. It looked like a red metal box with a screen on it. She held it out and began to move it around the area. First she aimed it at a Caterpie sitting on a tree branch. A Kakuna hung from the same branch, so she aimed it at Kakuna, too.

"What's that?" May asked.

"A Capture Styler," Solana explained.

"I've never heard of it," Max said.

"A Capture Styler lets me check on things like a Pokémon's abilities or its condition," she said. "This data is very helpful to a Pokémon Ranger. It allows us to figure out which Pokémon we can get help from."

Brock looked over her shoulder, nodding. "Cutting edge," he said.

Solana pointed the Capture Styler at three sleek, furry Pokémon on the forest floor.

"These Linoone seem to be the only ones who can use Slash," she said, studying the screen. She took a small gadget from the styler. It looked something like a metal top. She tossed it toward the Linoone.

"Capture On!" she yelled.

The device spun around the Linoone, leaving a path of light in its wake. The light circled the three Linoone.

Then Solana pulled a stylus from the Capture Styler. She pointed the stylus at the light.

"*Hiiii-yaaaaaaa!*" she yelled. She waved the stylus in a circle. The light around the Linoone spun faster and faster.

"Now what?" Ash asked.

"She's capturing them," Max informed him.

"Capturing?" May wondered out loud. She thought the only way to capture a Pokémon was with a Poké Ball.

"*Hiiii-yaaaaaa!*" Solana gave a final yell. Then she lowered the stylus.

The circle of light washed over the Linoone, then faded. The three Pokémon looked confused for a moment. Then they all faced Solana, ready for action.

"*Line!*" the Linoone cried.

Solana grinned. "Capture complete!"

Team Rocket — Trapped!

Solana turned to her Plusle. "Plusle, Helping Hand!" she called out.

"*Plus!*" Plusle replied. The Pokémon began to wave its hands, cheering on the Linoone.

"Do Slash, Linoone," Solana told the Pokémon.

The three Linoone slashed away at the vines with their sharp claws.

"*Line! Line! Line!*" They swiftly cut a path through the forest.

Ash was amazed. "They opened it right up!"

"So now they're *her* Pokémon?" May asked.

"No, that's not what 'capturing' means," Brock

explained. "Capturing allows you to use the Pokémon's abilities when you need them."

May understood. She looked at Solana. "So you were only *borrowing* the Pokémon to help out with what was needed!"

"Right," Solana said. "We'd better get going now, since Celebi's bound to be somewhere up ahead."

"All right!" Ash agreed. He headed down the newly cut trail. "We're coming, Pikachu!"

Not far away, Pikachu raced underneath the tangle of vines. It knew what it was looking for, and it wasn't far now.

Then Pikachu found it. Celebi lay on the forest floor, its eyes closed. Its normal bright green color was dull. Pikachu knew it needed help.

Pikachu ran up to Celebi. "*Pika!*" it cried.

Celebi weakly opened its eyes. It moaned in pain and began to close its eyes again.

But Pikachu knew Celebi had to stay awake. "*Pika! Pika!*" it urged.

Celebi smiled weakly.

Pikachu had an idea. "*Pikachu,*" it told Celebi. The little yellow Pokémon wanted Celebi to know it would be right back.

Then Pikachu ran off.

Nearby, Ash and the others hiked behind Solana. The Linoone slashed at the vines to clear their way.

"The other night, these vines started growing like crazy," Solana explained as they walked. "The Ranger Union got a call from the Cycling Organization, and they sent me to investigate."

"These vines are from Celebi?" May asked.

"The Rangers have heard the rumors of amazing vine growth associated with Celebi's appearance many times in the past," Solana replied. "But we've never had any real proof to go on. I'm fairly certain that Celebi's here now, but something bad may have happened."

Brock nodded. "*That* would explain why

Pikachu took off into the forest like that," he said.

"Pikachu's picked up on those things before," May pointed out.

Ash knew they were right. "Yeah! Pikachu must be looking for Celebi."

"Do you mind if we just keep this to ourselves?" Solana asked. "Celebi's a Legendary Pokémon, and I don't want to attract any attention."

"Don't worry about a thing," Ash said. "We won't tell anybody!"

"Uh, Twerp Group?"

Ash stopped. That voice sounded familiar. He looked up.

Jessie, James, and Meowth were tangled up in the vines! So was Jessie's big blue Pokémon, Wobbuffet.

"A small favor . . ." Jessie began.

"Would you mind . . ." James continued.

"Poppin' da top on dese vines for us?" Meowth finished.

Ash couldn't believe it. "Team Rocket!" he cried. "What are you guys doing here?"

May glared at them. "Of course I'm sure you're up to no good!" she said.

"Perish the thought!" James protested. "It's not like we were plotting a Twerp attack with an ambush to boot. . . ."

James realized his mistake too late. The bridge closing and the robot Officer Jenny had all been part of Team Rocket's plan to ambush Ash and his friends and steal Pikachu. And it would have worked, too, if they hadn't gotten tangled up in vines.

"Oops," James said weakly.

"Ambush?" Max asked angrily.

"Well, we can't just leave them like this," Solana said. "Linoone, help them out!"

"*Line! Line! Line!*"
The Linoone quickly cut through the vines.

"*Aaaaaaaah!*" Jessie, James, and Meowth cried out as they tumbled onto the forest floor.

"Thank you, Linoone," Solana said.

Team Rocket was bruised but happy.

"We're saved!" Meowth exclaimed. "Vine-free!"

"I thought it was our last ambush," James said.

"We *haven't* plotted our last plot," Jessie cheered.

"*Wobbuffet!*" added Jessie's Pokémon.

"Now I'm putting all of you on notice," Solana said sternly. "This forest is off-limits! Please leave here at once!"

Jessie, James, Meowth, and Wobbuffet all jumped to their feet.

"Bye-bye!" they cried.

Then Team Rocket ran back down the path.

Capture On!

Pikachu searched the forest for Poké berries. He knew the tasty pink fruits would help Celebi feel better.

Pikachu held out a berry. "*Pika! Pika!*" Pikachu told Celebi. It wanted the Pokémon to eat.

"*Bee,*" Celebi responded weakly. It took a tiny bite of the berry.

"*Pika?*" Pikachu asked. It hoped Celebi liked the fruit.

Celebi nodded its head. "*Celebi.*"

Ash and the others were closer now. But the vines were so thick that even Slash could not cut them.

"Thank you for all your help," Solana told the Linoone. They nodded and ran back into the woods.

The friends stared at the thick vines.

"What do we do?" May asked.

"We do another Pokémon capture!" Solana replied.

She scanned the ground with her Capture Styler. One Diglett and a Dugtrio popped up out of the dirt. Diglett was brown and wormlike, with a round pink nose. Dugtrio looked like three Diglett stuck together.

"We're asking you for your help," Solana told the Pokémon. "Capture On!"

Solana threw the spinning top at the Pokémon, and it circled them with white light. Then she pointed her Capture Styler at them.

"*Hiiii-yaaaaa!*" she yelled. She moved the styler in a circle.

The spinning light grew brighter and brighter. Then it lit up the Diglett and Dugtrio. They turned to Solana, waiting for instructions.

"Capture complete!" Solana yelled. "Plusle, Helping Hand!"

"*Plus! Plus! Plus!*" Plusle launched into a cheer once again.

Solana turned to the Ground-type Pokémon she had captured. "Diglett, Dugtrio, dig a hole!" she ordered.

The Pokémon ducked back underground. Then they furiously began to tunnel. Dirt flew out as they worked.

"Perfect!" Brock said. "We can use that hole as a shortcut to find Celebi."

"Correct!" Solana told him. "Okay, everybody, follow me!"

Solana jumped into the deep hole, and

Plusle jumped after her. One by one, Ash and his friends jumped in, too.

At the other end of the tunnel, Celebi was feeling a little better. Pikachu made funny faces to cheer up the Pokémon.

"*Diglett!*"

"*Dugtrio!*"

The Ground-type Pokémon popped out of the ground in front of Celebi. Solana appeared behind them.

"There you are, Celebi!" she cried happily.

Pikachu jumped in front of Celebi. Sparks sizzled on its cheeks. It would not let anyone hurt Celebi.

Then Ash climbed out of the tunnel.

"Pikachu!" he said.

Pikachu ran and jumped into Ash's arms. "*Pika! Pi!*"

"Man, was I worried," Ash said. He hugged Pikachu tightly. "I'm glad you're okay."

Max, May, and Brock climbed out next. Max

walked up to Celebi and knelt down to get a closer look.

"It's a Celebi — for real!" Max said.

"Wow, it's so cute," cooed May.

May looked up Celebi in the Pokédex. The small handheld device stored information about all kinds of Pokémon. A picture of Celebi appeared on the screen.

"Celebi, the Time Travel Pokémon," the Pokédex said. "Celebi wanders across time as Guardian of the Forest. Wherever it appears, trees and grass flourish."

Celebi's wide eyes looked at them, worried.

"Celebi, we're friends of yours, and we've come here to help you," Solana assured it.

"*Plusle!*" Her little Pokémon waved hello.

"*Bee?*" Celebi still wasn't sure.

"Like Pikachu did," Ash explained.

Celebi smiled. "*Celebi!*"

Solana did not want to move Celebi very far. They all set up camp in the woods. Solana put Celebi on a soft blanket on the forest floor.

Everyone sat in a circle around Celebi, watching the Pokémon sleep. A campfire flickered in the background, lighting up the dark forest.

Solana scanned Celebi with her Capture Styler. The Pokémon seemed to be healing nicely.

"That's great," the Pokémon Ranger said, looking at the screen. "A good night's sleep and Celebi will feel just fine."

"Awesome," May said.

"Hey, guys, isn't Celebi able to time travel?" Max asked.

"What's time travel?" May wondered out loud.

"It's when you have the power to travel into the past or future," he explained. He looked down at the sleeping Pokémon. "And I'll bet Celebi came here from a different time from ours."

"Most likely. Celebi might have been trying to get out of trouble and was injured in the forest," Solana guessed. "Perhaps all these vines were created as some sort of protection while Celebi was trying to heal!"

Ash looked down at Celebi. The Pokémon wasn't any bigger than Pikachu, but it had such amazing powers!

He hoped Celebi would be fine in the morning.

Better . . . and Worse!

Ash slept peacefully through the night in his sleeping bag, with Pikachu curled up next to him.

Then the cry of a Pokémon awakened him.

"*Celebi!*"

Ash sat up, startled. Was Celebi okay?

"*Celebi! Bee! Bee!*"

Celebi flew over the campsite, smiling. Morning sunlight streamed through the trees. Ash grinned. Celebi was all better!

"Celebi!" Ash cried happily.

The others woke up as well.

"Looks like that good night's sleep did the trick," May remarked.

Celebi swooped and twirled happily above them. Everyone climbed out of their sleeping bags to watch.

Soon Celebi's body began to glow with green light. Celebi flew over the thick vines, and they began to glow with light, too.

The friends watched in amazement as the vines all faded away. They transformed into droplets of shimmering light. The shining droplets floated up into the sky.

"The vines are disappearing," Max said.

"Celebi doesn't need them anymore," Brock explained.

Everyone smiled as Celebi flew happily around the forest. The little Pokémon flew straight up in the air. It whirled around. Then it gracefully floated down toward the ground.

Suddenly, something else appeared in the sky.

A big metal claw shot out of nowhere. The claw opened up, then clamped down, trapping Celebi inside.

The Pokémon was terrified.

"*Celebi!*" it cried out.

Thunder Wave, Plusle!

The metal arm was attached to a huge, metal Mecha Robot shaped like a giant Meowth!

Voices came out of the robot.

"Prepare for trouble, we're the cleanup crew!

With an ambush custom-made for you.

An evil as old as the galaxy.

Sent here to fulfill our destiny!"

The door on the Meowth head opened to reveal the cockpit where Jessie, James, and Meowth sat.

Meowth waved. "Meowth! Dat's me!"

Then Team Rocket launched into their motto.

"To denounce the evils of truth and love," said Jessie.

"To extend our reach to the stars above," James said.

"Jessie!"

"James!"

"Meowth's da name!"

"Whenever there's peace in the universe," Jessie said.

"Team Rocket . . ." said James.

"Is there . . ." said Meowth.

"To make everything worse!" cried Team Rocket.

Then Wobbuffet popped up. "*Wobbuffet!*"

"*Mime! Mime!*" piped James's little pink Pokémon, Mime Jr.

Solana was really angry. "I told them all to leave!"

"What do you want with Celebi?" Brock called out.

Jessie sneered. "Duh! Any Guardian of the Forest is going to be worth big bucks in the protection biz."

"So we'll gift that rascal to the Boss, and it'll ultimately become guardian of Team Rocket," James added. Mime Jr. sat on his lap.

"Then you know what happens," Meowth said.

Jessie, James, and Meowth chanted together. "We're good to go and flush with dough. Yo ho!"

Mime Jr. chanted along. "*Mime, Mime, Mime, Mime, Mime, Mime!*"

"*Wobbuffet!*" cried the big blue Pokémon.

"Now it's time ta blow!" Meowth announced.

"With Celebi in tow," Team Rocket said together.

The Mecha Robot began to stomp away across the forest. Celebi cried out in alarm.

"Come back!" Ash yelled.

Solana sprang into action. She ran after the Mecha. Then she jumped up and grabbed a tree branch with both hands. She swung her body around the branch like a gymnast, and hurled herself onto a higher branch. Plusle clung to her the whole time.

Next Solana grabbed some long vines growing from a tree. She swung herself up, up, up, then landed on the robot's head.

"Celebi, you're coming with me!" she told the Pokémon.

"*Cele!*" Celebi was happy to see her.

Ash smiled. "She's great!" he said admiringly.

"Pokémon Rangers are sure in good shape," May agreed.

"Thunder Wave, Plusle!" Solana cried.

Plusle nodded. It jumped off Solana's shoulder. She leaped off the robot's head and clung to the robot arm, right underneath Celebi.

Bright sparks shot from Plusle's body as it prepared for its attack. Then . . .

Bam! Plusle zapped the robot with a huge electric branch.

"*Eeeeek!*" Jessie, James, and Meowth shrieked as the electric charge coursed through them.

The controls on the robot began to sizzle and spark.

"Dat Plusle's power is gonna make dis bucket of bolts go ka-plooey!" Meowth said.

Solana swung over to the metal claw. She opened the claw and freed Celebi.

"It's all right," Solana assured Celebi. "Out you go!"

"*Celebi!*" The Pokémon cried happily. It quickly flew out. Then Solana and Plusle jumped off the robot to safety.

Jessie, James, Meowth, Wobbuffet, and Mime Jr. shook and shivered in the robot's cockpit.

"Yipes! We're stuck. Frozen stiff. Like ice!" Jessie, James, and Meowth said.

The robot began to shake and tremble.

Boom! The Mecha exploded. Team Rocket and their Pokémon flew high up into the air.

"Oh, poo! We're still frozen," Jessie said.

"And it's cold up there!" James cried, as they went up and up and up . . . and then they fell straight down, down, down, until . . .

Wham! They landed on the ground.

But Team Rocket wasn't out yet. They jumped to their feet.

"I, for one, feel much better," Meowth said.

Jessie and James each brandished a Poké Ball.

"You've zapped your last zap," Jessie threatened.

"You think you can thwart us just because you put out forest fires?" James taunted.

"Mime, Mime!" Mime Jr. copied James.

Solana stepped forward. Her eyes narrowed with anger.

"That is not funny!" she fumed. "I've had it!"

Ash stepped in front of her. "Hold on," he said. "We can take care of these guys for you."

"Sure," Brock said, stepping beside Ash. "We're getting good at it by now!"

Volt Tackle!

Jessie and James tossed out their Poké Balls.

"Okay, Seviper, prove them wrong!" Jessie cried. A large Poison-type Pokémon appeared. Black scales shimmered on its long body, and sharp fangs gleamed in its mouth.

"Cacnea, show them who's boss!" James yelled.

A green Pokémon covered with sharp spikes popped out — and immediately jumped on James, hugging him!

"I know *I'm* the boss," James yelped. "But you've got to show *them*. Go!"

"*Mime!*" Mime Jr. chimed in.

James tossed Cacnea in front of him. Seviper and Cacnea faced Ash and Brock, ready to attack. Pikachu jumped in front of Ash.

"Marshtomp, I choose you!" Brock yelled. He threw out a Poké Ball. A thick blue Water-type Pokémon popped out. It stood on two legs, glaring across the clearing at its opponents.

"*Marsh!*" it cried.

Team Rocket made the first move.

"Seviper, use Poison Tail!" Jessie ordered.

Seviper lunged across the field, whipping its tail at Marshtomp. But the Water-type Pokémon darted out of the way.

"Cacnea, use Pin Missile!" James cried.

"*Cacnea!*" Hundreds of sharp needles shot from Cacnea's round body. The needles flew at Pikachu, but the Electric-type Pokémon dodged the attack.

"Pikachu, Thunderbolt!" Ash yelled.

"Marshtomp, Mud Shot, let's go!" Brock cried.

Pikachu and Marshtomp both charged across the clearing.

"*Pikachuuu!*" Pikachu zapped Cacnea with a lightning bolt of energy.

"*Marsh!*" Marshtomp opened its mouth and shot a stream of mud into Seviper, sending the Pokémon tumbling backward.

"Now, Pikachu, Iron Tail!" Ash called out.

Pikachu somersaulted in the air. Its tail glowed bright white. Then . . . *SLAM!* It knocked its tail into Cacnea.

Cacnea went flying back, crashing into James.

"But I'm the good guy!" James wailed.

Ash knew the end was in sight. "Finish with Volt Tackle!"

It was a risky move. Pikachu hadn't perfected the attack yet. But Ash had a hunch. . . .

"*Pikaaaaaaaa!*" Pikachu charged across the field at super speed, building up energy as it ran. Its body was a ball of flaming energy by the time Pikachu reached its goal.

BOOM! Pikachu slammed into Team Rocket with tremendous force.

"Yeah! It worked, Pikachu!" Ash cheered.

Jessie, James, Meowth, Wobbuffet, and Mime Jr. sailed high into the sky.

"Back ta bein' an ice cube!" Meowth wailed.

Cacnea clung to James's chest with its sharp spikes. "This Cacnea-pop is sticking to me!" James yelled.

"No Celebi, no money, nothing but a bad case of brain freeze!" Jessie moaned.

"We're blasting off again!" Team Rocket cried.

Ash picked up Pikachu. He was really proud of his Pokémon.

"You rock, Pikachu!" he said.

"*Pika!*" Pikachu replied happily.

The remains of the Mecha Robot began to spark again. Without warning, a ball of flames burst from the charred metal. The fire flew into the nearby trees. They began to burn out of control.

"Oh no!" May cried. "The forest is going to burn up!"

Heal Bell

Celebi closed its eyes and flew toward the flames.

Then the Pokémon began to glow.

"*Celebiiiiii . . .*" The Pokémon's voice filled the air as light washed over the burning trees. Immediately, the flames transformed into thick vines. The vines wrapped around the trees.

"I guess Celebi isn't the only thing those vines were created to protect," Brock remarked.

Soon all of the flames had been transformed. Celebi nodded, and the vines dissolved. Shimmering droplets of light vanished into the blue sky.

Only the charred and burned trees were left. But Celebi wasn't finished yet. It shut its eyes, then concentrated on the trees.

Ash and the others watched in amazement as pulsating waves of light poured from Celebi's body. Along with the light came a sound . . . the beautiful, deep sound of a chiming bell.

"That sound! It's so pretty," May said.

Solana nodded. "I know. It's called Heal Bell."

The light and sound bathed the damaged trees. As if by magic, the trees slowly became healthy and green once again.

May shook her head in amazement. "Celebi's power is awesome."

"Celebi *is* Guardian of the Forest," Max agreed.

The light faded, and so did the sound of the bell. Now the sound of tinkling chimes rippled across the trees.

The trees stood tall and green, as good as new.

Celebi flew toward the friends. The Pokémon hovered above them.

"*Celebi!*" it said, thanking them.

"*Pika! Pika!*" Pikachu answered.

Ash smiled. It was funny how things had worked out. They had saved Celebi — and Celebi, in turn, had saved the forest.

"Thanks a lot, Celebi!" he called out.

Celebi nodded. Then it closed its eyes. A bright white light surrounded Celebi's body.

Celebi slowly began to rise high into the sky. The light grew brighter and brighter. Then it exploded. Everyone had to shield their eyes.

When the light faded, Celebi was gone.

"More time travel, right?" May guessed.

"Yup," Ash nodded.

"*Pika!*" Pikachu waved up at the sky.

"Wherever home is, I'm sure Celebi's glad to be back," Brock said, smiling.

Solana talked into her radio. "Solana here. Mission accomplished. Celebi's returned safely."

Max felt a little sad. "I wanted to play with Celebi a little longer," he said.

"I feel the same way, too," May said.

"You'll get to see Celebi again," Ash said confidently.

May and Max looked at Ash in surprise. Ash wasn't sure how he knew, but deep in his heart he did.

"We're all gonna see Celebi again," Ash said. "I know it . . . wait and see!"

"*Pika pi!*" Pikachu knew it, too.

And from somewhere in time, Celebi called out to them.

"*Celebiiiiiii . . .*"